KU-638-265

CONTENTS

BATMAN

While still a boy, Bruce Wayne watched his parents die at the hands of a petty criminal. After that tragic day, the young billionaire vowed to rid Gotham City of evil and keep its people safe. To achieve this goal, he trained his mind and body to become the World's Greatest Detective. Donning a costume inspired by a fearful run-in with bats at a young age, the Dark Knight now aims to strike the same sense of fear into his foes. But the Caped Crusader doesn't always work alone. He often teams up with other crime fighters, including Robin, Batgirl, Batwing, Batwoman and even . . . Mystery Inc.

THE MYSTERY INC. GANG

Travelling in a van called the Mystery Machine, these meddling kids, and their crime-fighting canine, solve mysteries all over the country – even in Gotham City!

TRAPPED IN CLOWN CASTLE

by Michael Anthony Steele
illustrated by Dario Brizuela

Batman created by Bob Kane with Bill Finger

raintree

a Capstone company — publishers for children

Raintree is an imprint of Capstone Global Library Limited, a company incorporated in England and Wales having its registered office at 264 Banbury Road, Oxford, OX2 7DY – Registered company number: 6695582

www.raintree.co.uk
myorders@raintree.co.uk

Designed by Tracy Davies
Originated by Capstone Global Library Ltd
Printed and bound in India

978 1 3982 4746 8

British Library Cataloguing in Publication Data
A full catalogue record for this book is available from the British Library.

THE MYSTERY INC. GANG

Scooby-Doo

A happy hound with a super snout, Scooby-Doo is the mascot of Mystery Inc. He'll do anything for a Scooby Snack!

Shaggy Rogers

Shaggy is a laid-back dude who would rather search for food than clues . . . but he usually finds both!

Fred Jones, Jr

Fred is the oldest member of the group. Friendly and fun-loving, he's a good sport — and good at them too.

Velma Dinkley

Velma is clever and book smart. She may be the youngest member of the team, but she's an old pro at cracking cases.

Daphne Blake

Brainy and bold, the fashion-forward Daphne solves mysteries with street smarts and a sense of style.

CHAPTER 1

SEND IN THE CLOWN

"Can we open our eyes yet?" Daphne asked as she opened the passenger door of the Mystery Machine.

"Not yet," Fred replied as he helped his friends step out of the van. "Just a little longer."

"This is so exciting," Velma said.

Shaggy stumbled out of the van. "Like, I hope you're not taking us to some kind of haunted house or something."

"Reah!" Scooby-Doo agreed as he followed Shaggy.

Fred laughed. "Nothing like that," he said. "In fact, you can all open your eyes now!"

The Mystery Inc. gang opened their eyes to an unusual sight. They stood in front of a large castle right in the middle of Gotham City. Moving spotlights washed over the dark stonework as they shone into the night sky.

"Hey," Shaggy said. "Like, a haunted castle is way worse than a haunted house!"

"It's not haunted," Fred said. "This is Clown Castle, home of one of my childhood favourites, Rizzo the Clown. I used to watch his TV show every Saturday morning when I was little."

Velma adjusted her glasses. "I heard about this place," she said. "After Rizzo died, the Gotham City Historical Society planned to turn this into a historical landmark."

"That's right," Fred agreed. He pointed to the queue of people waiting to get inside. "And I knew we couldn't miss opening night!" He led the way as they moved towards the queue.

"It's not raunted, right?" Scooby asked.

Daphne laughed and patted Scooby-Doo on the head. "Don't worry, I'm sure we'll have fun anyway."

After the group waited in the queue for a bit, they finally made it through the grand front door. One of the tour guides greeted them inside a large entrance hall.

"Welcome to Clown Castle," the young woman said. "It may seem a little luxurious, but Rizzo the Clown wanted a home fit for the greatest clown in the world."

POOF!

A burst of confetti erupted from somewhere above them.

"Good old Rizzo," Fred said with a chuckle as the coloured scraps of paper fluttered down upon the group. "He really loved his confetti."

The tour guide led the gang up a flight of stairs and then down a long landing with giant paintings in fancy frames. Each one showed a life-sized portrait of Rizzo himself. One painting featured the clown holding a rubber chicken. In another, Rizzo climbed out of a tiny car. Another painting had him holding a large custard pie with a lit fuse on top.

"These show some of Rizzo's most famous gags," the guide explained.

"Oh, boy," Fred said, pointing up at the paintings. "There's *Keep on Cluckin'*, *The Yuck Stops Here* and *Clown Commando!*"

As the tour guide led them along the landing, Scooby-Doo noticed that the eyes in one of the paintings seemed to follow them.

"Raggy," he said as he tugged on the back of Shaggy's shirt. "Rat painting is watching us!"

Shaggy spun around and squinted up at the nearest painting. It looked completely normal.

"Like, quit fooling around, Scoob," Shaggy said. "This place isn't supposed to be haunted, remember?"

"Rokay," Scooby replied. He glanced up at the painting one more time as the group walked along the landing. It looked normal again.

The tour guide led them into a chamber full of various items in glass cases. "These are some of Rizzo's favourite props," the woman said. "Over here are his juggling pins, his seltzer bottle and his giant lollipop."

"Oh, wow," Fred said as he moved towards the bottle on display. "Rizzo used to blast his guests with bubbly water from this very bottle."

"I'd stay back," the tour guide warned.

Fred felt his footstep trigger something in the floor. Suddenly, a hole appeared in the wall nearby.

WHOMP!

A pie shot out of the hole and hurtled towards Fred's face. He ducked at the last second and the pie flew over his head. But . . .

SPLAT!

. . . it hit Velma square in the face.

"Since Rizzo believed he was the greatest clown in the world, he wanted the greatest security system in the world," the guide continued.

Fred shook his head and laughed. "Classic Rizzo."

Velma slowly removed her glasses and glared at Fred. "Yes, hilarious."

Scooby-Doo rushed in to save the day.

SLUUUURRRRP! He cleaned her face and glasses with one long lick of his tongue.

"Thanks, Scooby," she said as she put her glasses back on.

Shaggy began stamping on the floor, looking for more hidden switches. "Like, now it's my turn. I love pie!"

Just then a creepy laugh echoed throughout the castle.

HA-HA-HA-HA-HA-HA-HA-HA-HA-HA!

"What kind of joke is that?" Daphne asked.

The tour guide shrugged. "I don't know. I've never heard that before." She led the way to a railing overlooking the main entrance hall.

Below them several other tour groups looked around in confusion as the spooky laugh filled the air once more.

HA-HA-HA-HA-HA-HA-HA-HA-HA-HA!

Just then, an eerie figure appeared at the railing on the level above them. Dressed in a tattered clown costume, the figure glowed bright green and looked like Rizzo himself.

Shaggy's hand shook as he pointed at the figure. "Like, is th-th-that the g-g-ghost of Rizzo the Clown?"

"Don't be silly, Shaggy," Velma replied. "Ghosts aren't real."

"Rooks real to me," Scooby-Doo said as his whole body quivered.

"I bet it's all part of the tour," Fred suggested. "Isn't that right?" he asked the tour guide. But she wasn't there.

The young woman had run down to the main entrance hall. She quickly joined the rest of the guests and other tour guides as they stampeded towards the exit. As soon as the last person was through the door, it slammed shut.

SLAM-SLAM! SLAM! SLAM-SLAM!

Shutters banged shut over each and every window. The people were gone. The ghost was gone. Only Mystery Inc. remained.

"Like, we're trapped in a creepy haunted castle that Fred absolutely assured me wasn't haunted!" Shaggy shouted.

"Don't worry, Shaggy," Velma said. "We'll get to the bottom of this."

Shaggy shook his head. "He's gonna say it. He's gonna say it."

"Well, gang," Fred said, "it looks like we have a real mystery on our hands!"

Shaggy's shoulders slumped. "And . . . he said it."

Daphne's eyes lit up with excitement. "Let's finish the tour and look for clues," she suggested.

The gang went back along the prop displays and moved through a doorway at the end. They found themselves in a tall, round room surrounded by clown horns attached to metal stands.

"Rizzo loved to play lullabies on his horns," Fred said as he squeezed the ball at the end of one of them. **Honk!**

Daphne squeezed another. **HONK!**

"Hey, you're right," she said, examining the horns. "They play different notes."

Shaggy hugged Scooby-Doo in fear. "Like, shouldn't we be quiet so the ghost thinks we left with everyone else?" he asked.

Daphne didn't listen. Instead, she squeezed three of the horns to play the tune "Twinkle, Twinkle, Little Star".

Honk-honk. Honk-honk. Honk-honk. Honk.

No sooner had she played the last note than a door slid shut behind them. High above them, the ceiling slid open to reveal a glass skylight above a giant spinning fan. Stars twinkled in the night sky.

"Hey, that's a neat trick," Velma said.

"Like, what's so neat about being trapped in a shrinking room?" Shaggy asked.

"Shrinking?" Fred asked.

"Reah," Scooby agreed. "Rook!" He pointed up at the fan and skylight. They moved closer and closer.

"The room's not shrinking," Velma said. "The floor is rising!"

"Moving us closer to those spinning fan blades," Fred added.

Daphne began honking other horns. "Maybe I can play a song to make it stop."

No matter what she tried, the floor kept pushing them closer to the fan above. The blades came closer and closer.

WHOOSH-WHOOSH-WHOOSH-WHOOSH!

Suddenly, a dark figure appeared outside the skylight. It grew closer until it finally broke through the glass. **KRASH!** The gang stepped aside as glass rained down from above.

"It's Batman!" Daphne shouted.

The crime fighter's cape fluttered behind him as he flung a Batarang at the fan. The sharp weapon jammed against one of the blades, causing it to stop spinning long enough for him to glide past. He landed on the rising floor in the middle of the group.

"Boy are we glad to see you," Fred said.

The Dark Knight glanced around the room. "What's going on here?"

Velma quickly explained how the horns triggered the rising floor.

"I tried other songs," Daphne explained. "But nothing else works."

"Hmm . . . ," Batman said, squinting his eyes. "Have you tried more of the same song?"

"No!" Daphne said before returning to the horns. She quickly played the next part of "Twinkle, Twinkle, Little Star."

Honk-honk. Honk-honk. Honk-honk. Honk.

Everyone jerked as the floor came to a stop. It slowly lowered back into position.

"We're saved!" Shaggy shouted.

HA-HA-HA-HA-HA-HA-HA-HA-HA-HA!

The spooky laugh came from somewhere in the castle.

Shaggy gulped. "Or maybe not."

HAVING A BALL

When the floor finally returned to normal, the first door opened again along with one on the other side of the room.

"Great!" Shaggy said. "Like, let's get out of this crazy castle!"

"Roo said it," Scooby-Doo agreed.

"Not so fast, you two," Velma said, blocking the door. "We still have a mystery to solve."

"And now we have the World's Greatest Detective on our team," Daphne added.

She, Fred and Velma took turns telling Batman about the strange goings-on in the castle, including the appearance of Rizzo's ghost.

Batman's lips tightened. "Since there are no such things as ghosts, there must be someone behind all this."

Velma smiled and rocked back on her heels. "That's what I always say."

Fred raised a finger. "I say we split up and look for clues," he suggested.

"Like, normally I hate it when he says that," Shaggy said. "But this time, I call Batman's team!"

"Me too!" Scooby added, raising a paw.

"All right," Batman said. "Stay behind me."

"Like, that's the safest place to be," Shaggy agreed.

Fred, Velma and Daphne exited through one door. Shaggy and Scooby-Doo followed Batman through the other. Just as Batman had told them, Shaggy and Scooby stayed close behind as he explored the dark castle corridors.

Batman reached the end of a corridor and pushed open two large doors. The room beyond was a grand dining room surrounded by several life-sized toy soldier statues. A long table stretched across the room. It was filled with all kinds of food.

Shaggy and Scooby-Doo's mouths fell open at the sight. They shook their heads, coming out of their daze, and then shot past the crime fighter.

"I thought I told you to stay behind me," the Dark Knight said.

"That's okay, Mister Batman, sir," Shaggy said. "You are the World's Greatest Detective, but Scoob and I are the world's greatest gobblers!"

"Reah!" Scooby-Doo agreed as he tied a napkin around his neck.

As the two friends sat down, strange noises erupted from their seats.

FFFT-FFFFFFFT!

Shaggy gave an embarrassed giggle. Then he reached down and pulled out a deflated whoopee cushion.

"Would you look at that, Scoob," Shaggy said. "That Rizzo got us again."

Scooby-Doo didn't answer. Instead, he grabbed a great big hamburger with both paws. He went to take a bite, but he couldn't chew through it. He chewed and chewed but nothing happened. Scooby finally pulled the burger out of the bun and flopped it back and forth.

WUBBA-WUBBA-WUBBA!

"A rubber ramburger?" Scooby asked.

Meanwhile, Shaggy's teeth clenched the end of a hot dog. He pulled and pulled but the hot dog stretched longer and longer. It slipped out his hands and . . . **SMAK!** The hot dog hit his face like a big rubber band.

"Like, what's the big idea?" Shaggy asked. "This is all joke food!"

Scooby-Doo unscrewed a jar of peanuts and . . . **BOING!** A giant toy snake sprang out.

Scooby shook his head. "Rot funny."

"Let's keep moving," Batman said. "There aren't any clues here."

Just then, the toy soldiers came to life. They reached out and ran towards the Dark Knight. Batman kicked one of them away and then backflipped onto the table. Shaggy and Scooby ducked under the table as the soldiers moved in. The crime fighter dodged blows from his foes while landing several punches and kicks.

While Batman battled the soldiers, Shaggy and Scooby reached up onto the table to try out more food.

Shaggy spit out a mouthful of popcorn. "Pop Rocks in the popcorn?" he said.

As Scooby-Doo sipped from a glass, water dribbled out of his mouth.

"And dribble glasses?" Shaggy asked. "Like, what kind of ditzy dinner is this?"

When the room fell silent, Shaggy and Scooby scooted out from under the table. All of the toy soldiers were scattered around the room. Some of them were in pieces.

"I was wrong," Batman said as he examined an arm with sparking wires poking out from the end. "These were remote-controlled robots. That's a clue."

"I hope the others are having better luck finding clues than we are," Fred said as he, Daphne and Velma explored the third floor of the castle. They crept down a dark corridor until they reached a set of stairs winding down into darkness.

"I wonder where these stairs go," Daphne said.

Velma shrugged. "They go down. Come on," she said as she led the way down the stairs.

The group had only gone down a few steps when all the stairs dropped at once, creating a smooth ramp. The three screamed as they slid down and around and around. They finally shot out of the end and landed in a large room filled with thousands of colourful plastic balls.

As they all bobbed to the surface, Fred giggled with joy. "A silly slide into a ball pit? What a classic Rizzo prank!"

Velma adjusted her glasses and then jumped with surprise. "Well, Fred, if you like it so much you can tell him."

"Tell who?" Fred asked.

Daphne's finger shook as she pointed to a glowing figure jutting out of the other side of the ball pit. "The ghost of Rizzo the Clown!"

HA-HA-HA-HA-HA-HA-HA-HA-HA-HA!

The ghost gave a ghoulish laugh before ducking under the colourful balls. Fred, Daphne and Velma spread out, trying to move away from where they spotted the ghost.

The ghost suddenly popped up next to Daphne. "Peek-a-boo!" Rizzo shouted.

"Yikes!" Daphne screamed as she scrambled to get away.

The ghost dropped down and then popped up next to Fred. "I see you!" he yelled.

"Ah!" Fred shouted as the ghost reached out for him. He ducked under the balls before the clown could catch him.

The three friends moved around the pit wondering where the ghost would pop up next. Luckily, when he did appear, it was on the other side of the room. Unluckily, he reached out and pulled a long lever. The balls began to swirl around and around the room, carrying the gang with them. Then the balls began funnelling down a drain in the centre of the room.

"Grab onto something," Fred said as he latched onto the handrail near the stairs. When Daphne came around, he reached out and snatched her hand. The two held tight against the swirling balls.

Meanwhile, the ghost put his hands together and dived into the centre of the pit. He disappeared among the spinning balls.

"Where's Velma?" Daphne asked.

Fred scanned the whirling balls. "I can't see her anywhere."

"Velma!" Daphne shouted.

The last of the balls disappeared into a large hole in the centre of the floor. A round hatch rose into place, sealing it shut. Fred and Daphne were alone. The ghost and Velma were gone.

CHAPTER 3

TEETH FOR TWO

Fred and Daphne quickly found another set of stairs leading out of the empty ball pit. They made their way through the castle until they met up with Batman, Shaggy and Scooby-Doo.

"Rhere's Velma?" Scooby asked.

"The ghost got her," Fred replied.

"Zoinks!" Shaggy shouted. He glanced around in fright. "Like, the ghost is taking prisoners now?!!"

"Don't worry," Batman said. "We'll find her and whoever's behind all this."

The Dark Knight led the way as they moved deeper into the castle. They turned a corner and another long corridor stretched out before them. Batman halted.

"Wait here," he ordered. "It could be a trap."

The Dark Knight took two steps into the dark corridor before his boot triggered a switch on the floor.

WHOMP!

A pie shot out of the wall, and Batman ducked just in time. The pie zoomed over his head and hit the wall behind him.

SPLAT!

The crime fighter examined the floor. "There are remote switches along this entire corridor," he said. "Step where I step, to avoid them."

"Like, Mister Batman, sir," Shaggy said. "Scoob and I have this one covered."

"Reah!" Scooby agreed.

"After all, we've been training for this our whole lives," Shaggy continued. He reached a hand towards Scooby. "Shall we, buddy-ol' pal?"

"Ree shall," Scooby agreed as he put his paw in Shaggy's hand. Shaggy jerked the dog into a graceful spin down the corridor. Shaggy danced after him.

WHOMP! WHOMP-WHOMP! WHOMP!

Pies shot from every direction, but the two friends gobbled them down as fast as they came. They danced down the corridor, stepping on switch after switch.

WHOMP-WHOMP! WHOMP! WHOMP!

The pies kept coming and they kept eating.

WHOMP! WHOMP!

Shaggy gobbled up one pie, did a somersault, and ate another before he hit the floor.

WHOMP-WHOMP-WHOMP!

Scooby-Doo caught three pies with his paws. He stacked them neatly before swallowing the entire set in one gulp.

The two ended their routine at the other end of the corridor. Shaggy rubbed his belly as Scooby brushed a few crumbs from his fur.

"Like, all clear," Shaggy announced.

"And ree-ricious!" Scooby-Doo said, licking his lips.

Batman led the others past Shaggy and Scooby and through the door at the other end. After some more exploring, the group soon found themselves standing on a balcony overlooking a deep, dark pit.

"Is this a dead end?" Daphne asked.

"No, look!" Fred pointed to another balcony and door on the opposite side. A thin tightrope stretched between the two balconies.

TK-TK-TK-TK-TK-TK-TK-TK!

A strange clicking sound filled the air.

"Like, what's that noise?" Shaggy asked. "Are you so scared your teeth are chattering, Scoob?"

Scooby-Doo looked over the railing. "Not my teeth. Rook!"

Everyone followed his gaze to the bottom of the pit. It was buzzing with dozens of giant chattering teeth. The snapping jaws piled on top of each other as they jumped into the air.

"Boy, if the fall doesn't get you, those teeth will," Fred said.

Batman pulled out a Batarang. "There's a lever over there labelled *bridge*," he said. "I think I can . . ."

"Wait a minute," Daphne said as she spotted a unicycle on the balcony. "I'll take care of this one." She hopped onto the unicycle and pedalled out onto the tightrope.

The rest of the gang watched nervously as Daphne inched across the thin line.

"Those circus arts classes are finally going to pay off!" she said as she pedalled.

When she finally made it to the other balcony, the door opened. Out stepped the glowing ghost of Rizzo the Clown.

"Jeepers!" Daphne shouted.

"Knock, knock?" asked Rizzo.

Daphne shrugged while trying to keep her balance. "Who's there?"

"Summers," replied the ghost.

Daphne wobbled some more. "Summers who?"

"Summer's over," replied the clown with a chuckle. "Have a nice Fall!"

As the ghost burst into laughter, Daphne finally lost her balance. She reached out for something to grab, but only snagged the colourful handkerchief from Rizzo's jacket pocket. The ghost laughed harder as she pulled out the long line of handkerchiefs, all tied together. When she got to the last one, she lost her balance completely and fell towards the chattering teeth.

POP!

Batman fired his grapnel and it latched onto the wall high above them. He swung out, ready to catch Daphne. But before he got there, a secret panel opened in the wall below. A shadowy figure reached out with a huge net and caught Daphne before she reached the bottom. The figure pulled her back through the panel, and it shut before the crime fighter got there.

CHAPTER 4

SURROUND CLOWN

Batman swung onto the opposite balcony. Just like Daphne, the ghost of Rizzo was gone too. The crime fighter pulled the lever, and a thin platform shot out from under the balcony. The bridge stretched across the pit to what was left of the Mystery Inc. gang.

"Who was that?" Fred asked. "Who caught Daphne?"

Batman shook his head. "I don't know. But it seems as if this so-called *ghost* isn't working alone."

"Like, one ghost isn't bad enough?" Shaggy asked.

"I still don't believe in ghosts," Batman said. "And if there is more than one person behind this, then that's another clue."

Batman took the lead as they moved up a set of stairs that led to another strange room in Clown Castle. This time they entered a large maze of mirrors. The angled mirrors and glass panels made it difficult to work out what was real and what was a reflection.

"Not a mirror maze," Fred said, shaking his head. "I must say, I'm getting pretty tired of Rizzo's pranks."

"Stay close," Batman ordered. "It'll be very easy to get lost in here."

As the group snaked through the maze, their reflections surrounded them and moved in different directions.

Scooby-Doo giggled. "Four Raggys."

"That's right, Scoob," Shaggy said. "And four Scoobys, four Freds, four Batmans and *one* ghost of Rizzo the Clown." Shaggy shook his head. "Zoinks! One ghost of Rizzo the Clown?!!"

The ghost let out another chilling laugh.

HA-HA-HA-HA-HA-HA-HA-HA-HA-HA!

With lightning speed, Batman whirled a Batarang towards the ghost.

WHHP-KRAK!

The clown only laughed harder when the weapon struck and cracked a mirror. It was only a reflection. The ghost stepped to the side, disappearing from view. Then, suddenly, four ghosts appeared around them.

Batman threw punches, kicks and more Batarangs at the ghosts, but they were still only reflections.

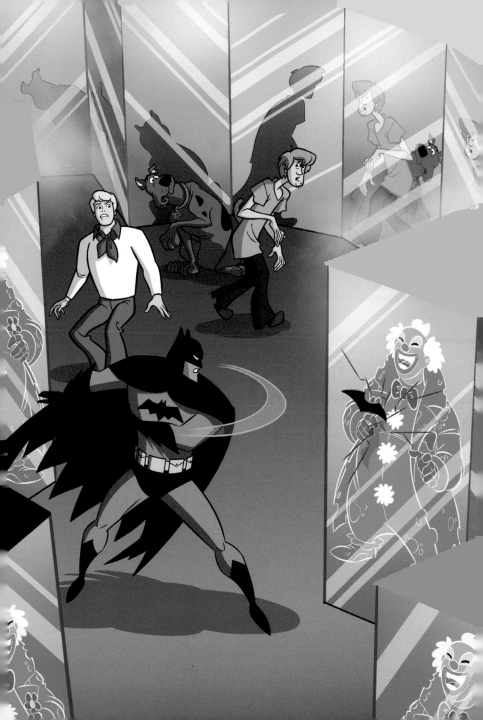

"Like, let's get out of here!" Shaggy shouted.

He and Scooby ran off in different directions. Unfortunately, they both kept smacking into glass panels. **BAM! SMAK! BAM!** They couldn't find their way out of the maze.

"Calm down, guys," Fred warned. "They're just reflections." He reached out to the Rizzo closest to him. "See? They can't . . ." Fred's hand landed on the jacket of the very *real* ghost of Rizzo the Clown. Fred gulped. "Uh-oh."

"Smell the pretty flower," Rizzo said as he leaned closer.

PSSST!

The flower on the clown's jacket squirted liquid onto Fred's face. Fred coughed and spluttered before something in the liquid knocked him out cold. The clown caught Fred and threw him over his shoulder. He carried him out of the maze.

"He got Fred!" Shaggy shouted. "Like, what do we do now?"

"Same as before," Batman replied. "We find the others and find out who's behind all this."

Batman led them out of the shattered maze. As the three explored the castle, they came across many rooms they'd already visited. The corridor of portraits, the dining hall, the empty ball pit – the rest of the gang was nowhere to be found.

Batman finally led them to a room they hadn't seen yet. They stepped inside a large hall lined with statues of different kinds of clowns. There was a court jester, a jack-in-the-box, a mime and even a rodeo clown.

"Like, I'm really getting tired of clowns," Shaggy said, glancing at the surrounding figures.

"Reah," Scooby agreed.

Just then, the creepy laugh filled the air once more.

HA-HA-HA-HA-HA-HA-HA-HA-HA-HA!

"Be ready for anything," Batman warned. "There's no telling what . . ." His voice trailed off as he looked back at Shaggy and Scooby. They weren't there. Instead, there were two new clown statues in the hall. Shaggy and Scooby-Doo were dressed as rodeo clowns, standing perfectly still at the end of the long line of clown statues.

Shaggy shrugged. "Like, if you can't beat 'em, join 'em?" he whispered.

BAM!

A large wooden door at the other end of the room shook as something struck the other side.

BAM! BAM!

It shuddered harder, rattling on its hinges.

Ka-BLAM!

The door exploded outwards as a giant beast burst out. It was a vicious bull with a ring in its nose and long, sharp horns. Batman somersaulted over the animal as it charged. It galloped right for Shaggy and Scooby-Doo.

"Zoinks!" Shaggy shouted. "Like, did we pick the wrong costumes or what?"

"Roo said it," Scooby agreed as they scrambled out of the way.

The bull skidded to a stop and spun around. It pawed at the floor with one of its hooves before charging at Shaggy and Scooby again.

The Dark Knight swooped in and landed between the friends and the approaching beast. He grabbed the bull by the horns and planted his boots. The animal pushed Batman across the floor before whipping its head to one side. The crime fighter was flung away as the beast kept charging.

Shaggy and Scooby-Doo shivered as they hugged each other.

"Like, I guess this is goodbye, Scoob-ol'-pal," Shaggy said.

Scooby whimpered. "Roodbye, Raggy."

Before the bull made it to them, Batman dashed forward and landed a flying kick to the side of the beast. **WHAM!** The animal skidded across the floor before coming apart in two pieces. The front half of the bull went one way and the back half went the other. It wasn't a real animal at all.

A muffled laugh came from the front half of the bull. That half stood and a familiar figure stepped out of the costume. It was Rizzo!

"It's the rhost!" Scooby said.

"Not a ghost," Batman corrected. "The clues we've gathered point towards two very sinister jokesters."

"Right as usual, Bat-brains," Rizzo said. He reached up and pulled off a rubber mask. Another painted face was underneath.

"Like, it's Gotham City super criminal, the Joker," Shaggy said.

"Don't forget about me," said another voice, as the back half of the bull stood up. The costume dropped to reveal a woman wearing a black and red costume.

"And Harley Quinn," Shaggy continued.

HA-HA-HA-HA-HA-HA-HA-HA-HA-HA!

The Joker gave the most sinister laugh yet.

CHAPTER 5

SWEET SURPRISE

Batman clenched his fists. "What are you up to, Joker?"

The Clown Prince of Crime gave a chuckle. "Why, Batsy! You don't think I'd sit quietly while someone else claimed to be the greatest clown in the world, did you?"

Harley crossed her arms. "Yeah," she agreed. "Everyone knows that Mister J is the greatest!"

The Joker rolled his eyes. "Yes, yes, Harley, we all got that."

Harley drooped with disappointment.

"What did you do with the others?" Batman asked.

"I'm so glad you asked," the criminal replied with a grin. "Because they're set to be part of my greatest joke yet. I just need a few more ingredients."

"What are those?" Shaggy asked.

"Why, all of you, of course," the Joker replied before glancing around. "You know, even though I prefer my ha-hacienda, Rizzo did collect some wonderful toys in this castle."

Harley pulled out a box with a long antenna. She pressed a button and the surrounding statues came to life. The criminals cackled with laughter as robotic clowns rushed in to attack.

"Zoinks!" Shaggy shouted as he ducked under grabbing hands. "Like, it's gone clown crazy in here!"

Scooby-Doo scrambled away from two more of the robots. "Really razy!"

Batman grabbed the arm of the court jester and flipped it over his head. It slammed into the mime and rodeo clown. The Dark Knight was about to punch another attacking robot when the jack-in-the-box struck, wrapping around him like a snake.

Batman locked eyes with Shaggy and Scooby. "Get out of here!" he ordered.

Before the hero could break free from the coils, the rest of the clowns swarmed him. They piled onto him like tackling rugby players.

"You don't have to tell us twice," Shaggy said as he and Scooby bolted for the exit.

The friends ran away from the brawl, down a long corridor, and up three flights of stairs. They finally stopped in an empty corridor to catch their breath.

"Like, what are we going to do, Scoob?" Shaggy asked. "The Joker has our friends *and* Batman!"

Scooby-Doo took a deep breath. "Ree have to help!"

Shaggy's shoulders slumped. "I was afraid you were going to say that." Shaggy took a deep breath too. "All right, pal. We have to be brave."

"Reah," Scooby agreed.

"Like, we have to be strong."

Scooby-Doo nodded his head. "Reah!"

"And not fall for any more of the Joker's traps," Shaggy continued.

"Reah!" Scooby agreed again. "Reah! Reah!"

That was when the trap door opened beneath their feet.

FWOP!

The two friends screamed as they dropped down and slid inside a long, clear tube. The pipe soon split, and Shaggy and Scooby went in different directions.

Their tubes looped, zigzagged, and spiralled. They were both still screaming when they dropped from the pipes and landed on two comfy chairs. Even though Shaggy and Scooby had stopped moving, their eyes kept spinning.

Shaggy shook his head and glanced around. His eyes widened when he saw what was laid out before them. "Like, what kind of clown craziness now?"

His and Scooby's chairs faced the strangest thing yet in Clown Castle. A giant custard pie sat on a huge coiled spring. The pie was surrounded by an odd collection of toys, tools and unusual contraptions. Worse yet, the rest of the Mystery Inc. gang and Batman were strapped to the top of the enormous pie.

"Welcome, welcome!" said the Joker. He and Harley Quinn stood off to the side of the strange set-up. "Every good clown needs an audience, am I right?"

"You're so right, Mister J," Harley agreed, clapping her hands.

"Like, what's with all the stuff?" Shaggy asked.

"I'm so glad you asked, my boy," the Joker replied. "You see, anybody can splat someone's face with a pie. But splatting a pie full of faces? Now, *that's* funny!"

Harley pointed to the brick wall with a large target painted on it. Several pieces of giant crust and bits of pie filling were strewn about.

"And as you can see, the test pies went off without a hitch," she said.

"And the funniest part of all is how the pie is triggered," the Joker said.

The villain turned and pointed to the surrounding contraption. "See, I pull this rope, releasing the bowling ball. It rolls down the ramp, hitting the dominoes. They fall down in a row, the last one releasing the balloon that rises up and switches on the fan . . ."

Shaggy and Scooby had trouble keeping up as the Joker explained the complicated collection of gadgets.

The Joker ended his explanation with a little monkey sitting on a stationary bicycle in front of a window blind. ". . . and when the string pulls the blind, the monkey sees the banana on the other side. The monkey pedals the bike, flipping the switch and releasing the pie."

Shaggy scratched his head. "Like, wouldn't it be easier just to pull the blind first?" he asked.

"Shaggy!" shouted Velma and Daphne.

"Raggy!" shouted Scooby-Doo.

Shaggy shrugged. "What?"

The Joker frowned. "Easier isn't funny."

"Don't do this, Joker," Batman ordered.

"Yeah," Fred agreed. "Shouldn't some jokes be, I don't know, left to the imagination?"

The Joker paused. "Hmm . . . maybe. But not my style." Then he pulled the rope, and the bowling ball began to roll.

Shaggy sprang from his seat. He tried to stop the bowling ball, but he was too late. The ball hit the pins, and they started the row of dominoes. Shaggy stumbled over parts of the machine, trying to stop the reaction, but he was always too late.

The Joker and Harley Quinn roared with laughter as Shaggy kept trying.

"Oh, my," the Joker said. "This is funnier than I'd planned. I'm a genius."

Shaggy couldn't get to the balloon in time, so it rose up and switched on the fan. Shaggy switched off the fan, but he was too late again. It had already blown the blades of a toy windmill. The windmill set off another part of the contraption.

The criminals laughed harder and harder as Shaggy was always too late to stop the machine.

Fortunately, they were so busy laughing that they didn't spot Scooby-Doo as he sneaked out of his seat. The dog crept over and freed Batman and the others.

Shaggy crashed through the machine, still one step behind it every time. He finally gave up when a flowerpot fell from a shelf. It pulled a rope that raised the blind in front of the monkey. "Oh, no," Shaggy said. "I'm too late."

But the monkey didn't pedal. The banana was gone.

The Joker fumed with rage. "Where's my banana?!!"

"Rover here," Scooby-Doo said as he held the banana in one paw.

The Joker and Harley Quinn were so furious that they didn't even notice everyone had been freed. They charged towards Scooby. The dog squeezed the banana, shooting it out of its peel and up to the monkey. He then dropped the banana peel and took off running.

Harley stepped on the slippery skin and skidded across the floor. She smacked into the Joker and they flew towards the pie. *Splat!* They landed on top just as the monkey began pedalling.

BOING!

The spring shot the pie towards the wall.

Ka-SPLAT!

The pie and criminals smacked into the wall. They groaned as they slowly slid to the floor.

Batman marched over and cuffed the two pie-covered criminals. "They'll wake up back in Arkham Asylum, where they belong."

"I think I've had enough clown antics to last a lifetime," Fred said. Then he shook his head and chuckled. "But slipping on a banana peel? That was a classic Rizzo prank too."

"Like, way to go, Scoob," Shaggy said.

Scooby-Doo giggled. "Rooby-dooby doo!"

THE JOKER

Real Name: Unknown

Occupation: Professional criminal

Base: Gotham City

Height: 1.95 metres

Weight: 87 kilograms

Eyes: Green

Hair: Green

Powers/Abilities: Genius-level intelligence, chemistry and engineering skills

Biography: The Clown Prince of Crime. The Ace of Knaves. Batman's most dangerous enemy is known by many names, but he answers to no one. After falling into a vat of toxic waste, this once lowly criminal was transformed into an evil madman. The chemical bath bleached his skin, dyed his hair green, and peeled back his lips into a permanent grin. Since then, the Joker has had only one purpose in life: to destroy Batman. In the meantime, he's happy tormenting the people of Gotham City.

- The Clown Prince of Crime has spent more time in Arkham Asylum than any Gotham City criminal. But that doesn't mean he's comfortable behind bars. He has also escaped more times than anyone.

- While at Arkham, the Joker met Dr Harleen Quinzel. She fell in love with the crazy clown and aided in his many escapes. Soon, she turned to a life of crime herself, as the evil jester Harley Quinn.

- Always the trickster, the Joker designs all of his weapons to look comical in order to conceal their true danger. This trickery usually gets a chuckle or two from his foes, giving the Joker an opportunity to strike first.

BIOGRAPHIES

photo by M. A. Steele

Michael Anthony Steele has been in the entertainment industry for more than 28 years, writing for television, films and video games. He has authored more than 120 books for exciting characters and brands, including Batman, Superman, Wonder Woman, Spider-Man, Shrek, Scooby-Doo, WISHBONE, LEGO City, Garfield, Night at the Museum and The Penguins of Madagascar. Steele lives on a ranch in Texas, USA, but he enjoys meeting his readers when he visits schools and libraries all across the United States.

photo by Dario Brizuela

Dario Brizuela works traditionally and digitally in many different illustration styles. His work can be found in a wide range of properties, including Star Wars Tales, DC Super Hero Girls, DC Super Friends, Transformers, Scooby-Doo! Team-Up and more. Brizuela lives in Buenos Aires, Argentina.

GLOSSARY

antenna wire that sends or receives radio waves

contraption strange or odd device or machine

grapnel grappling hook connected to a rope that can be fired like a gun

hacienda Spanish name for the main house on an estate

jester entertainer at a court in the Middle Ages

luxurious expensive and beautiful

mime performer who expresses himself or herself without words

prop item used by an actor or performer during a show

seltzer sparkling water

sinister seeming evil and threatening

stampede run in panic

unicycle vehicle with pedals like a bicycle but with only one wheel and no handlebars

THINK ABOUT IT

1. Rizzo the Clown is one of Fred's favourite TV stars from childhood. Who is your favourite TV or film star and why?

2. When the gang splits up, Shaggy and Scooby go with Batman because they think he will keep them safe. Would you have gone with Batman too? Or would you have joined Fred, Daphne and Velma? Explain your answer.

3. Why does the Joker take over Clown Castle? What do you think he and Harley would have turned the location into if Batman and the Mystery Inc. gang hadn't captured them?

WRITE ABOUT IT

1. The Joker and Harley Quinn create a series of traps to capture Batman and the Mystery Inc. gang. Which trap did you like the best? Write a paragraph explaining which one you liked and why.

2. The Joker creates a chain-reaction contraption to set off his giant pie trap. If you could create your own chain-reaction contraption, what would it include? Draw a picture of it and write a paragraph about what it would do.

3. At the end of the story, Batman cuffs the pie-covered Joker and Harley Quinn. What happens next? Write a new chapter describing how he takes them to Arkham Asylum or how they escape. You decide!

READ THEM ALL!